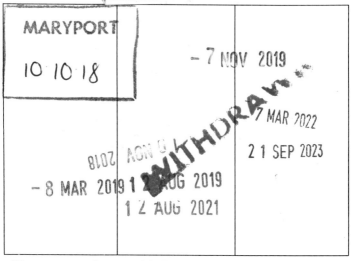

To Freya

Special thanks to
Karen Ball

ORCHARD BOOKS

First published in Great Britain in 2018 by The Watts Publishing Group

1 3 5 7 9 10 8 6 4 2

© 2018 Rainbow Magic Limited.
© 2018 HIT Entertainment Limited.
Illustrations © Orchard Books 2018

HiT entertainment

A CIP catalogue record for this book is available from the British Library.

ISBN 978 1 40835 498 8

Printed and bound in Great Britain by CPI Group (UK) Ltd, Croydon, CR0 4YY

MIX
Paper from
responsible sources
FSC® C104740
www.fsc.org

The paper and board used in this book are made from wood from responsible sources

Orchard Books
An imprint of Hachette Children's Group
Part of The Watts Publishing Group Limited
Carmelite House, 50 Victoria Embankment, London EC4Y 0DZ

An Hachette UK Company
www.hachette.co.uk
www.hachettechildrens.co.uk

Chelsea
the Chimpanzee
Fairy

by Daisy Meadows

ORCHARD

www.rainbowmagicbooks.co.uk

Fairyland Palace

Sparkle Forest

Snow Leopard Enclosure

The Girls' Cabin

Elephant Bath

TAIL AND TRUNK SAFARI PARK

Jack Frost's
Ice Castle

Blue Ice
Mountains

Giraffe Junction

POLAR
ZONE

The Polar Bear Enclosure

Cheeky Chimp
Corner

TAIL AND TRUNK SAFARI PARK

Jack Frost's Spell

I want a zoo – don't say I'm wrong!
But finding pets takes far too long.
Fill each cage with stinky straw.
I will get what I'm wishing for!

In Sparkle Forest every day,
Peculiar creatures run and play.
The animals are rare – so what?
Get in there and steal the lot!

Contents

Chapter One
One Bounching Bobo

"Do you think they've noticed us?"
Rachel Walker asked as she and her best
friend, Kirsty, watched a chimpanzee
high up in a tree.

"I hope not," said Kirsty Tate,
whispering. "I want to see them play."

They were on their third day at Tail
and Trunk Safari Park and the park

manager, Ahmed, had brought them here
to see the mischief that the chimpanzees
got up to at Cheeky Chimp Corner – the
ape enclosure. There was a long wooden
bench beneath some trees. Earlier that
morning, Rachel and Kirsty had helped
Ahmed put out grapes, bananas and nuts
for the animals. Then they'd gone back
to Ahmed's truck, which was painted in
orange and black tiger stripes.

Now, the girls sat in the back with a
fluffy zebra-print blanket over their knees.
Ahmed had passed them each a fruit
smoothie that he'd made earlier.

"Grapes and kiwi fruit, mixed with
yogurt and almond milk," he said. "Drink
up!"

The girls each took a sip through pink
and yellow striped paper straws.

"Yum!" Kirsty said.

"Delicious," Rachel said, taking another sip.

The two of them were best friends. They'd come to this safari park with Rachel's parents, Mr and Mrs Walker. They were staying in a little wooden hut with gingham curtains and they had offered to help Ahmed around the park. The two girls would get up extra early each morning, to help the park manager change the animals' straw and put out fresh food for them. It was a magical start to the day, before the park gates opened to visitors. Magic seemed to follow the two best friends around wherever they went.

Ahmed was watching the chimpanzees carefully, his hat tipped back on his head. "Did you know ..." he began to say. Rachel and Kirsty shared a secret glance and smiled. "... chimpanzees share ninety-eight per cent of their DNA with humans." Ahmed loved his facts, even more than he loved the animals of Tail and Trunk Safari Park.

Suddenly, the back of the truck gave a lurch. Rachel nearly dropped her smoothie! There was a scrabbling sound as something ran away.

"What was that?" Ahmed cried, leaping out from behind the wheel. Kirsty and Rachel carefully placed their smoothies in the truck's cup holders and scrambled out after him. A tiny, hairy shape dragged its feet across the grass and heaved itself over the fence towards the Cheeky Chimp Corner. His furry little hands glowed in the morning sunshine, but it wasn't sunlight glinting off his fur. The glow looked almost magical.

"Oh no!" Rachel whispered, pulling Kirsty behind a tree. "I think it's Bouncy

Bobo. That glow – it looks like Jack Frost's magic."

Bouncy Bobo was a chimpanzee from Sparkle Forest in Fairyland. Rachel and Kirsty had gone there with Etta the Elephant Fairy, and they had met the rest of the Endangered Animals Fairies. At Sparkle Forest, all sorts of animals from around the world lived together in the forest glade, even ones that were endangered in Kirsty and Rachel's world. Then Jack Frost had arrived! With the help of his naughty goblins, he'd captured the four fairies' special magical animals – an elephant, a snow leopard, a polar bear … and Bobo, the bouncy chimpanzee. Rachel and Kirsty had helped get two of the animals back to Sparkle Forest, but there were still two more to save, and one of them was Bobo.

"What is that naughty chimpanzee doing?" Ahmed suddenly cried, pulling out his phone to take photos. "We don't like to see the animals stealing. Wait till I tell the park owner about this!"

Bobo had dragged himself up onto the chimpanzees' picnic table and stole a

banana out of another chimpanzee's fist.
But straight away, the banana slipped out
of his grasp. Then, he grabbed a bunch of
grapes off another ape and ran as fast as
he could towards a climbing frame. He
heaved himself up the wooden poles and
greedily tried to shove the grapes into his
mouth — but he kept missing! The fruit
fell and splattered on the
ground and the
creature yowled
with hunger.

"Jack Frost
has made
his hands
all slippery,"
Rachel said,
peering out
from behind the

tree. "Now Bobo can't feed himself! And without his usual bounce, I bet he can't get himself back to Sparkle Forest. He must really be missing Chelsea – poor Bobo!"

Kirsty nodded, making the little satin bows on the end of her pigtails bounce against her unicorn T-shirt. "Look!" she said. "What's he doing now?" She pointed as Bobo crept back down and ran over to a chimpanzee who was sleeping on a log, to steal her kiwi fruit! She woke up and opened her mouth in a huge yawn, then froze, staring at Bobo. He tried to shove the whole kiwi fruit into his mouth, but with a *squelch!* it squeezed out of his hand and flew over his shoulder. The fruit landed in a messy heap on the ground.

"He's in big trouble now," Rachel said.

"Ahmed looks like he's going to burst!"
The park manager had run back to
the truck and leant inside to reach for
something. He lifted up a large brown
paper bag with lettering on the side.
Rachel and Kirsty went over and saw
that the letters spelt out: "Tail and Trunk
Treats".

"What do you have in there?" Kirsty
asked. A group of the chimpanzees were
wrestling on the ground now, rolling over
and over in the grass.

"More fruit!" Ahmed said, holding a
huge bunch of grapes up like a trophy.
His eyes glinted beneath the brim of his
safari hat. "We need to stop that chimp
spoiling all the food, or there'll be chaos.
I have a plan."

Rachel looked over at the ape

enclosure, where the animals were squabbling. A frown creased her brow. "Good," she said, "because I think we need one."

Chapter Two
The Grape Game

Bobo was going from chimpanzee to chimpanzee, trying to steal their snacks. The other animals each grabbed their fruit before he could eat it, but they were getting more and more wound up and were hooting with frustration.

"Do chimpanzees usually behave like this?" Rachel asked.

Ahmed shook his head. "Not usually," he said. "But apes are very possessive of their food. Don't worry, I think I know how to stop this. Here, hold out your hands!"

Kirsty and Rachel shared a
confused look, but they cupped their
hands and Ahmed tore off some
grapes for each of them.

"We can't go too near the
chimpanzees," he told the girls. "We need
to respect their space."

Rachel felt her smile
fade. If they couldn't
get near the animals,
how would they get
Bobo back to Sparkle
Forest?

"But we can do
something else," said
Ahmed. "Look!" He pulled his mobile
phone out again and showed them a
little video on the screen. It was of some
chimpanzees in a jungle and they were

tearing bark off trees in order to eat the
ants that hid beneath. "Chimpanzees
love finding hidden treats," he told them,
shoving his phone back into his pocket.
"So if we lay a trail, they'll follow. We'll
make food fun, rather than a reason
to fall out. Hopefully, they'll all stop
squabbling!"

"What fun!" Rachel cried, then
hesitated. "But what about Bobo? He
can't seem to feed himself."

"Don't worry," Ahmed reassured her.
"One of the zoo keepers will come and
feed him. For now, we just need to get
him away from the other animals."

Ahmed was tiptoeing from bush to
bush, leaving a grape here and another
there. "Come on, girls," he called back.

Rachel and Kirsty looked at each other.

"If we help Ahmed now, maybe we'll find a way of helping Bobo get back to Sparkle Forest," Kirsty said.

"It's a plan!" Rachel cried. She ran over to a wooden fence in front of the bushes

and carefully balanced a row of grapes
along the top. Kirsty skipped ahead of
her and dropped grapes, one by one, in
the long grass. It was like playing a game
of Hansel and Gretel, leaving a trail of
breadcrumbs out of the forest!

Kirsty looked back over her shoulder.
The chimpanzees had stopped wrestling

and were standing up on their hind legs,
sniffing the air. Their nostrils flared and
they started to hoot with excitement.

"I think they know that there are treats
waiting for them," Kirsty said. The three
of them ran to hide behind Ahmed's
truck. They poked their noses over the
side and watched. Ahmed had pulled a

little notebook out of his top pocket and licked the end of a stubby pencil.

"I shall make some scientific notes," he said, marking the date at the top of the first page. "We might be about to see something record-breaking."

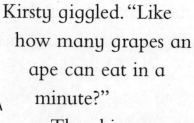

Kirsty giggled. "Like how many grapes an ape can eat in a minute?"

The chimpanzees were racing from bush to tree to fence, shoving grapes into their mouths. They'd forgotten all about their argument with Bobo. What a relief! Ahmed crept forwards for a closer look.

But as the animals raced past a bush,

28

Rachel spotted something she didn't like. She tapped Kirsty on the shoulder and pointed. "Look!" she whispered. Fortunately, Ahmed was too busy taking notes to see what she was pointing at. Two little green faces and two pairs of huge green feet poked out of the bush.

"It's Jack Frost's goblins!" Rachel said, trying to keep her voice quiet. "What are they doing here?"

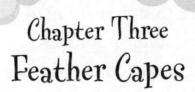

Chapter Three
Feather Capes

"Look! They're creeping up on Bobo," Rachel said. Bobo perched on the fence, plucking up grapes one by one. But the grapes kept slithering out of his hairy hands, which glimmered with Jack Frost's naughty magic. The chimpanzee was so busy trying to eat the grapes that he didn't notice two pairs of green feet shuffling from bush to bush.

"We have to stop them getting to Bobo first!" Kirsty said, "But how? If the goblins spot us, they'll tell Jack Frost that we're on to him."

Just then, there was a noise from the truck. Ahmed had left his backpack on the seat and the canvas was wriggling and glowing, as though something magical was inside. Rachel leant over and tugged on one end of the drawstring. The backpack burst open as a tiny, sparkling figure flew out in a cloud of fairy dust. Her wings glittered in rainbow colours as she turned a loop-the-loop through the air, coming to land on the truck's bonnet.

"Chelsea the Chimpanzee Fairy!"

Rachel and Kirsty
cried at the same
time. They'd met their
new fairy friend back
in Sparkle Forest.
She wore a pair of
snuggly fur bootees
and her hair bounced
around her cheeks as
she grinned at them.

"I'm so glad I
found you," she said,
smiling. "It's Bobo!
We think he's trapped
here …"

"He is!" Kirsty told her. "Jack Frost has
used his magic to stop Bobo from feeding
himself and now he doesn't have the
energy to get home. The goblins are here,

too." She pointed past Chelsea's shoulder, and the fairy turned round to see giant green feet poking out from behind a bush. A long, skinny hand was reaching towards Bobo.

"No!" Chelsea cried, flying into the air. "Stop that, you naughty goblins." She fluttered over and the girls ran after her, but it was too late. Bony green fingers wrapped around Bobo's tummy and there was a flash of blue light. Rachel and

Kirsty rubbed their eyes, and stared at the fence. Where Bobo had been sitting moments before, now there was just a small pile of grapes.

"I knew it!" Chelsea cried. "They've taken Bobo to Jack Frost. Will you help me save him?"

"Of course!" Rachel and Kirsty said, linking arms. They had gone on so many magical adventures together, they would never say no to helping a fairy.

Rachel looked over at Ahmed. He was still busy scribbling notes. "Let's go quickly," she said.

Chelsea waved her wand over the friends. A cloud of sparkles swirled around them as they shrank down and felt their bodies lift into the air. More sparkles fell down from the branches of a tree and they felt their shoulders grow

warm and tingly as with a *pop!* two pairs
of beautiful fairy wings sprang out from
between their shoulder blades.

The air shimmered and the trees of
the safari park melted away. The golden
yellow sun became a pale circle in the
sky. There was a sudden cold breeze and
giant snowflakes fell down around the
girls.

Their feet came down into a soft
pile of powdery snow. Rachel gave a
shiver. Ahead of them rose the walls of
Jack Frost's Ice Palace, with its turrets
and frozen moat. It looked cold and
unwelcoming.

"How could anyone call that place a
home?" Kirsty said, wrapping her arms
around her body for warmth. Chelsea
gave another wave of her wand and both

girls found themselves wearing snow-
white feathery capes that reached almost
to their ankles. Kirsty rested her cheek
against the feathers – they were so soft!

There was the sudden sound of
cheering from inside the palace.

"Come on," Chelsea said, bobbing in

the air. "Let's go and see what they're up to." The three of them flew over towards a tall window and perched on the icy windowsill to peer inside.

"Oh no!" Rachel gasped.

"I can't believe it!" Kirsty said, shaking her wings in frustration.

"Poor Bobo," Chelsea said, her eyes brimming with tears.

Chapter Four
Circus School

Chelsea's chimpanzee was sitting in a cage that was propped up on a stool, at the head of a table. All along the table were plates and dishes filled with quivering green jellies and yucky cold custard, wobbly-looking flans and green lemonade. The party food didn't look tasty at all!

Jack Frost was sitting at the other end of the table and raised a goblet carved from ice. All the goblins around the table cheered and did the same.

"To our chimpanzee's tea party!" Jack Frost said, laughing with delight. He took a big slurp, green liquid slopping all

down his tunic.

Bobo's head hung miserably, his chin touching his chest. The girls knew how much he loved his food. This didn't look like a good meal, even for a hungry chimpanzee.

"We'll get him out of there," Kirsty said, as she bobbed in the air. She and Rachel exchanged a high five. No way was Jack Frost getting away with this. "Come on!"

The three of them flew around the back of the palace. A kitchen window was open and they darted inside. The kitchen was in chaos!

Whoever had made the party food hadn't
done a very good job. Bags of flour spilt
out across the table. Beside them stood
a jar of what looked like frogspawn and
plates piled with rock cakes that had
been burnt in the oven. But seeing the
rock cakes gave Rachel an idea.

She reached for one and tossed it
towards Kirsty, who caught it neatly in
one hand.

"Can you remember that juggling class we went to?" Rachel asked.

Kirsty's eyes lit up with delight. "The circus school? That was so much fun!" she cried. She bent to pick up another rock cake and a fairy cake and the two girls began juggling the cakes between them.

Chelsea flew over to the kitchen door and rescued two red and white polka dot aprons. "Put these on," she said. "Jack Frost has never been in the palace kitchens, I'm sure. Tell him you're the Circus Chef party entertainers!"

Rachel tossed a rock cake to Kirsty, and Kirsty gently threw a fairy cake in return. "We can distract Jack Frost with our juggling," she said, "and Chelsea can get Bobo out of the cage. Deal?"

"Deal!" Chelsea and Rachel cried.

Quickly, Rachel and Kirsty put on the aprons, their wings poking out of the sides. Then they flew down the icy corridors towards the dining room. They burst through the door, just in time to see Jack Frost reaching through Bobo's cage to drape a paper garland around the chimpanzee's shoulders. Chelsea hid behind the door, her wings fluttering with anxiety. "Stop him," she whispered to the girls.

Rachel and Kirsty burst into the room and began juggling.

"We're the Circus Chef party entertainers!" Rachel said.

"We have won prizes for our juggling!" Kirsty cried. They had won third prize at Circus School.

Jack Frost froze to the spot, watching

them. Then he grinned, showing his yellow teeth. "This is the best party ever!" he said.

As he watched the girls juggling,
Chelsea flew over to Bobo's cage. She
touched her magic wand to the lock and
with a *ping!* the door sprang open and
Bobo climbed out.

Immediately, Bobo scrambled down
and began to bounce around the

room. He was so excited to be free again! Bounce, bounce, bounce! Then, with Chelsea chasing after him, the chimpanzee leapt out of the room. Bobo was bouncing all over the Ice Palace!

Chapter Five
A Fruit Tale

"Stop him!" cried Jack Frost, hopping from foot to foot. His goblins scrambled down off their stools and ran after Bobo, but they weren't quick enough. The chimpanzee swung from a chandelier. Then he leapt into the hallway and

tumbled up the grand staircase. He ran
from room to room, swinging around
bed posts and hanging from curtains,
screaming and smacking his lips.

"This is awful!" Jack Frost shouted up
the stairs. "He's ruining my Ice Palace."
Kirsty and Rachel had taken off their
spotty aprons. "You two!" Jack Frost
pointed a trembling green finger as he

finally recognised them. "I should have known you'd have something to do with it." Then he clutched his hands together in front of his bony chest. "Please," he whispered. "Get that animal out of my palace. He's ruining everything."

It looked like Jack Frost wasn't such an animal lover, after all.

Rachel looked up the stairs to where Bobo was jumping up and down on a pile of cushions. Feathers were being scattered everywhere! Chelsea was trying to calm him down but it was no good. She flew down the stairs to join them and glared at Jack Frost. His goblins hid behind him, peering out at her as she placed her fists on her hips.

"Now, do you see what you've done?" she said to Jack Frost. "When you put

animals in cages, you stop them from being themselves. Of course Bobo wants to bounce around. That's what he's meant to do!" Her little fairy cheeks were pink with racing after her chimpanzee. Rachel and Kirsty knew they had to stop this.

"I have an idea," Rachel said, remembering Ahmed's plan to stop the chimpanzees from fighting back at the

Tail and Trunk Safari Park. "Chelsea, could you magic up some delicious fruit?"

"Of course!" Chelsea said. She flew back into the dining room and waved her wand over the horrid green party food as she began to chant a spell:

Cold custard, green jelly,
Doesn't suit a hungry belly.

Tasty fruit is much more sweet,
Let's give this chimp a proper treat!

A trail of golden fairy dust fell over all the green food and turned it into platters of glistening fruit. And not just grapes! There were kiwis, blueberries, apples, raspberries and more.

"There's enough here for one of Ahmed's smoothies!" Kirsty cried, scooping up a handful of blueberries. She ran out in the hallway and lifted her hands up. "Look what I have!" she called up the stairs. "Mmmmm, tasty!"

Instantly, Bobo stopped bouncing on the cushions. He raised himself up and sniffed the air. He saw the fruit that Rachel and Kirsty were scattering down the corridor, towards the main door of the Ice Palace.

"Just get him out of here!" Jack Frost wailed from where he was perching on his ice throne.

Chelsea flew ahead and opened the door, waving her wand to create a circle of sparkles in the air. Bobo ran towards them, grabbing fruit off the floor, and bounded out of the Ice Palace as Kirsty and Rachel ran ahead, tossing bananas in the air.

Bobo shoved the tasty fruit into his mouth, eating happily. This time, none of the fruit slipped to the ground. Jack Frost's spell had been broken at last! Then

the ape gave
an extra-giant
leap, straight
into the cloud
of sparkles
that fell down
from Chelsea's
wand.

Kirsty and
Rachel felt the
glittering sparkles
rain down over them
too. Their feet started to leave the ground
as they felt their bodies lift into the air. A
sudden breeze carried them up and away
through a curtain of clouds. They were
heading back to Sparkle Forest!
Chelsea, Bobo, Rachel and Kirsty all

arrived back at Sparkle Forest, just as the midday sun was rising over the treetops. The animals and fairies all gathered in the glade to welcome them back and Bobo bounced around, giving big wet kisses to his friends.

Chapter Six
The Chimp Cafe

Etta the Elephant Fairy laughed and wiped the kiss from her cheek. "We're so glad to see Bobo back," she said.

Chelsea gave Rachel and Kirsty a hug. "I couldn't have done this without you. You're the best friends a fairy could have." She glanced up at the sky. "We should get you back home now, though."

Rachel and Kirsty looked around at the animals gathered in the glade. There were so many of them, and all sorts of animals that needed looking after – leopards and lions, bats and baboons, giraffes and geckos.

"We're happy to have helped again,"
Rachel said. "And we'll be back soon.
We know that Selma's snow leopard still
needs rescuing." It made her heart sad
to think about the leopard, separated
from his friends. She dipped in the air.

Her wings were
beginning to get
tired from all
the flying. For
now, it really
was time to get
home.

"Goodbye,
everyone!" Kirsty cried, waving her hand
above her head.

Chelsea blew them a kiss then circled
her wand. Everything seemed to shimmer
and blur and then Rachel and Kirsty

found themselves standing in long grass, beside the Cheeky Chimp Corner.

No time had passed at all. Ahmed was staring at the open flap of his backpack. "I thought I'd put a double knot in the drawstring," he said. He glanced up and saw the two friends. "Come on. I've

taken loads of notes on the chimpanzees. They're fascinating creatures!"

"They really are," Rachel said, as the three of them climbed into the truck. They began to drive through the safari park, back to their cabin. Mr and Mrs Walker had promised the girls that they'd

go swimming. They couldn't wait!

"There's just one animal left to save," Kirsty said, as they drove past some rhinos rolling about in mud. Selma still needed their help to get her snow leopard back to Sparkle Forest.

"Did you have a good time?" Mrs Walker asked, as they pulled up outside the cabin. Rachel and Kirsty clambered out and Ahmed gave them a wave, before driving off.

"It was really grape!" Kirsty said, grinning. "Not too much monkeying around."

Mrs Walker frowned. "Don't you mean great?" she asked.

Kirsty and Rachel couldn't hide their giggles as they looked at each other. "Something like that," Rachel told her

mum. Then the two of them ran inside
to find their swimming costumes and
goggles.

They knew that another magical
adventure was waiting for them, with one

more Endangered Animals Fairy needing their help. The two best friends would do everything they could to help the fairies. But for now, it was time to go for a swim!

The End

**Now it's time for Kirsty and
Rachel to help ...**

Selma the Snow Leopard Fairy

Read on for a sneak peek ...

Rachel Walker opened her eyes. It was
still dark in the room she was sharing
with her best friend, Kirsty Tate.

"What woke me up?" she wondered.

As if to answer her question, she heard
a few clear, beautiful notes from outside
the window.

"The dawn chorus," Rachel told herself,
smiling.

"Are you awake too?" came Kirsty's
voice from across the room.

Rachel sat up and turned on her lamp.

Kirsty hopped out of bed and came to sit beside her.

"Did the birdsong wake you up?" Rachel asked.

"No, I had a dream that we didn't find Dotty," said Kirsty. "We had to leave Tail and Trunk Safari Park without helping the fairies."

She shivered, and Rachel gave her a hug.

"That sounds more like a nightmare than a dream," she said. "But it's not going to come true. We'll find Dotty before we leave today. I'm sure of it."

The girls had won a night and a day at the safari park in a competition. Then they had persuaded Rachel's parents to stay for a few more days. They had been enjoying visiting the park with Ahmed, their guide, and helping to look after the animals. They had also been sharing a magical fairy adventure. Jack Frost had stolen the precious baby animals that belonged with the Endangered Animals Fairies. They had managed to find three of them, but Dotty the baby snow leopard was still missing.

"I don't feel tired at all," said Rachel. "Let's watch the sun come up, and then we'll think of a plan to start searching for Dotty."

The girls kneeled up and opened the curtains above Rachel's bed. The first light of the day was so white and bright that they had to turn away. But the room was bright and white too.

"There's a light coming from behind the dressing table," said Kirsty in astonishment.

As if dawn was breaking inside the

room, the light grew brighter. Then Selma the Snow Leopard Fairy appeared at the top of the dressing table.

"I'm glad you're both awake," she said. "I'm sorry it's so early, but I've come to ask for your help."

Selma shook back her golden-brown hair. She was wearing jeans and a summery green top with brown boots.

"We'll do whatever we can to help," said Rachel at once.

"Dawn and dusk are the best times to see snow leopards," Selma said. "That's why I thought it would be a good idea to start searching early. Will you come to the snow leopard enclosure and help me?"

"Of course we will," said Kirsty.

Quickly, the girls got dressed. Selma skipped into the air and flicked her wand. A shower of silvery sparkles rained around the girls.

"I feel as if I'm fizzing all over!" cried Rachel in delight.

Giggling, the best friends shrank to fairy size as their fairy wings appeared. They flew around the lampshade a few times, practising their dives and loop-the-loops.

"Being a fairy is the best," said Kirsty, plumping down on Rachel's pillow.

"Come on," said Rachel, pulling her into the air again. "Dotty needs our help."

The three fairies zoomed out of the window and into the fresh morning air. The safari park was quiet. No visitors were allowed in this early, and most of the keepers were still in bed. Every now and then, a peacock let out a shrill cry.

Everything else was still.

Rachel and Kirsty flew over the animal habitats.

"It's funny," said Kirsty. "At the start of the week, the safari park seemed like a big maze. Now I feel as if I'd know my way around it with a blindfold on."

"That's because you've been helping to take care of the animals every day," said Selma. "Looking after animals and their habitats is the best way to get to know them."

"There's the snow leopard enclosure," said Rachel, pointing down to the waterfall at the centre of the enclosure. "But I can't see a single snow leopard."

The rock walls around the waterfall were rugged and steep. They looked as bare and grey as the walls of Jack Frost's Castle. But Selma smiled.

"Look again," she said. "Snow leopards are good at hiding."

They flew closer, and suddenly Rachel glimpsed a rock with black spots all over it. Then she realised that it wasn't a rock at all.

"Oh my goodness," she said, laughing. "It's a snow leopard. I didn't know they were so good at blending in with the background."

"They're amazing at camouflage," said Selma in a proud voice. "But I wish Dotty wasn't so good at it. I can't see her here."

Just then, a loud voice broke the peace of the morning.

"Coming, ready or not!" it squawked.

"That sounds exactly like a goblin," said Kirsty.

A green head peeped around one side

of a pointy rock. From the other side, a fluffy white cub tumbled down, landed silently and scrambled away.

"Look at the tips of that cub's fur," said Rachel. "They've got a blue sparkle."

"Could that be Dotty?" Kirsty asked.

"It is Dotty," Selma exclaimed. "I'd know her markings anywhere."

Read Selma the Snow Leopard Fairy to find out what adventures are in store for Kirsty and Rachel!

Calling all parents, carers and teachers!
The Rainbow Magic fairies are here to help
your child enter the magical world of reading.
Whatever reading stage they are at, there's
a Rainbow Magic book for everyone!
Here is Lydia the Reading Fairy's guide to
supporting your child's journey at all levels.

(1)

Starting Out

Our Rainbow Magic Beginner Readers are perfect for first-time readers who are just beginning to develop reading skills and confidence. Approved by teachers, they contain a full range of educational levelling, as well as lively full-colour illustrations.

(2)

Developing Readers

Rainbow Magic Early Readers contain longer stories and wider vocabulary for building stamina and growing confidence. These are adaptations of our most popular Rainbow Magic stories, specially developed for younger readers in conjunction with an Early Years reading consultant, with full-colour illustrations.

(3)

Going Solo

The Rainbow Magic chapter books - a mixture of series and one-off specials - contain accessible writing to encourage your child to venture into reading independently. These highly collectible and much-loved magical stories inspire a love of reading to last a lifetime.

www.rainbowmagicbooks.co.uk

"Rainbow Magic got my daughter reading chapter books. Great sparkly covers, cute fairies and traditional stories full of magic that she found impossible to put down" - Mother of Edie (6 years)

"Florence LOVES the Rainbow Magic books. She really enjoys reading now" - Mother of Florence (6 years)

The Rainbow Magic Reading Challenge

Well done, fairy friend – you have completed the book!
This book was worth 5 points.

See how far you have climbed on the
Reading Rainbow opposite.

The more books you read, the more points you will get,
and the closer you will be to becoming a Fairy Princess!

How to get your Reading Rainbow
1. Cut out the coin below
2. Go to the Rainbow Magic website
3. Download and print out your poster
4. Add your coin and climb up the Reading Rainbow!

There's all this and lots more at
www.rainbowmagicbooks.co.uk

You'll find activities, competitions, stories, a special
newsletter and complete profiles of all the
Rainbow Magic fairies. Find a fairy with your name!